DINOSAURS' HALLOWEEN

by Liza Donnelly

To my mother

A LUCAS • EVANS BOOK

Library of Congress Cataloging-in-Publication Data

Donnelly, Liza.
Dinosaurs' halloween.

Summary: An encounter with a fellow trick-or-treater whose
dinosaur costume is remarkably realistic gives a boy a Halloween
full of surprises.
[1. Halloween — Fiction.   2. Dinosaurs — Fiction]   I. Title.
PZ7.D7195Di   1987   [E]   86-31552
ISBN 0-590-41025-3

12 11 10 9 8 7 6 5   9/8 0 1 2/9

Printed in the U.S.A.   23

First Scholastic printing, September 1987

"We'll have the best costumes on the block!"

"Now don't be scared. It's only Halloween."

"Trick or treat!"

"Thank you!"

"Oh, hi! What a neat costume!"

"Want to come with us?"

"Trick or treat!"

"Thank you!"

"Trick or treat!"

"We're getting great candy!"

"Hand it over!"

"Rip off his silly mask!"

"Now the mutt!"

"I'll get him!"

"Take the loot and run!"

*"See you next Halloween!"

"This was the best Halloween ever!"

GLOSSARY

ALLOSAURUS (AL-uh-sawr-us) This huge meat eater measured about 35 feet and walked on its powerful hind legs. Its large, hinged jaw was filled with razor-sharp teeth.

BRONTOSAURUS (BRON-tuh-sawr-us) A well-known plant eater, also called an apatosaurus, this giant four-legged dinosaur was 75 feet long from its nose to the end of its 30-foot tail. Its small, snouted head had a brain about the size of a human fist. Its 20-foot neck, longer than its body, enabled it to browse on the tops of trees.

DIMETRODON (dye-MET-ruh-don) Not a dinosaur, but a pelycosaur (lizard), the dimetrodon had a sail about three feet high along its back that might have helped to control its body temperature. About ten feet long, it was a four-legged meat eater.

MICROVENATOR (my-kro-ven-AY-tor) This turkey-sized dinosaur was only four feet long, including its tail, and weighed about 14 pounds. It had three long fingers on its short forearms; it probably ran quite swiftly on its strong hind legs.

MONSTERSAURUS (MON-ster-sawr-us) Not a dinosaur, but a monster, it is green with orange spots. It likes to live with dinosaurs in little boys' rooms.

PARASAUROLOPHUS (par-ah-sawr-OL-uh-fus) This plant-eating dinosaur had an unusual crest, a five-foot hollow tube on the back of its head. Its hands were webbed, and its beak was spoon-shaped. About 30 feet long, it walked on two legs.

POLACANTHUS (pol-luh-KANTH-us) A plant eater, this 15-foot dinosaur had two rows of spines that ran down its back. Triangular bony plates protected its tail.

PTERANODON (tair-AN-o-don) Not a dinosaur, but a pterosaur (winged lizard), this small creature had a long head that measured six feet from the tip of its pointy beak to the end of its bony crest on the back of its head. A fish eater, the pteranodon was probably more of a glider than a true flyer.

TRICERATOPS (try-SAIR-uh-tops) Three-horned face, this four-legged plant eater was about 25 feet long. It was very aggressive and well protected by huge brow horns, neck covering, and leathery skin. Triceratops was one of the last dinosaurs to die out.

TYLOSAURUS (TYE-lo-sawr-us) Not a dinosaur, but a mosasaur (seagoing lizard), this slim creature was 30 to 40 feet long. It had a huge jaw and was a savage hunter that ate fish and shellfish.